WHODUNNIT?

CAROLINE BROWNE

Story told by
Helen Cresswell

JONATHAN CAPE
THIRTY-TWO BEDFORD SQUARE
LONDON

This is the mystery of the Big Butterly Burglary. Can you help to solve it? If you are good at looking for clues, you can help. If not, just listen to the story.

It all started the day the Mouse family went down to the station to spot trains.

They made a day of it and took a picnic.
Tilly and Tom spotted plenty of trains, but
they spotted something else as well. All
mice are curiously curious, they love to
poke and pry.

So as soon as Tilly and Tom had gobbled their
cheese they poked and pried in the waiting room.
Behind the iron stove Tom spotted a bundle of
newspaper, and when they poked and pried into
that what should roll out but a sparkling ruby
ring!
What a spot!

Off they went to the police station.
P.C. Dog looked at the ring. "That is a worthless object," he proclaimed. "It isn't worth tuppence."
P.C. Dog couldn't see things even when they were right under his nose, let alone behind his left ear.

Tilly and Tom spotted something, though.
Can you?

P.C. Dog turned and looked at the notice. He did not turn a hair. "I knew at a glance that ring was worth a fortune," he said. "I'll get in touch with the Palace right away. Well done, young mice!"

Tilly and Tom had found the ring that had been stolen from the Princess herself!

"We're amazing!" they cried. "We're the champion spotters of the world!"

Off they ran. They wanted everyone in Butterly to hear the news.

The whole village was buzzing.
"What amazingly clever young mice!" everyone said.

The young voles were so jealous that they straightaway started looking for stolen rings in their garden.
"*We* can spot rings, too!" they squeaked.
They didn't though. They found a couple of empty flowerpots, a rubber ball and a bumble bee, but that was all.
Oh – and a snail. But I expect you've already spotted that.

The next day a gold-edged letter arrived. It said:

*The Princess wishes to thank
the clever young mice
who found her stolen ring.
She wishes the village of Butterly
to hold a fête in their honour
the day after tomorrow.
She herself will attend.*

*P.S. She hopes that by then
the Burglar will have
been caught.*

Soon the news was round the village. Everyone ran hither and thither. As many villagers as possible crowded into Granny Nanny's front room.
"We will hold the biggest and best fête in the history of Butterly," she told everyone. "But what about the Burglary? The question is – WHODUNNIT?"

"Whodunnit?" "Whodunnit?" The question went right round the village. Everyone wanted to solve the crime.

But everyone was also getting
ready for the fête.
Mrs Blackbird's choir were to sing a
special song to welcome the Princess.

If their eyes had been open half as wide as their mouths, they might have discovered then and there whodunnit.

Everyone in Butterly swept and polished and practised and hung out flags and whenever they had time to draw breath would gasp out the question "Whodunnit?"

Two of them even sat down to make a list of suspects.
"It must be somebody who went to town on the train last week," they said wisely. "Because that is where the Palace is."
They made the list:

1 Mr and Mrs Frog.

2 Mr Fox.

3 Mrs Rabbit.

4 Mr Rat.

Could it be Mr and Mrs Frog? They are toymakers, and go in for clocks as well. Every week they go on the train to town to buy bits and bobs for their work. At this very moment they are making a splendid doll's house.

"We'll give it to the Princess at the fête," said Mr Frog. "Then we shall be Toymakers by Royal Appointment!"

Could it be Mr Fox? He is an artist who specialises in portraits.
He goes to town on the train every week to buy paints and
brushes and have his whiskers trimmed.
At this very moment he is dreaming of the moment when he will
meet the Princess.
"I shall paint her portrait,"
he decides. "Then I shall be
Portrait Painter by Royal
Appointment!"

Could it be Mr Rat? He goes to town on the train every week to collect his wages. He is very poor, and dreams of being very rich. "Drat those young mice, finding that ring!" he thinks.

Could it be Mrs Rabbit? She is the village baker, and goes on the train to town every week to buy sugar and currants and treacle and jam. She doesn't *look* like a burglar, but then you can never tell! And in any case that day she finds that she, too, has been burgled!

After a meeting at Granny Nanny's the Mouse family went back to their attic. But when they got there they found everything topsy-turvy.
"*We've* been burgled!"

Tilly and Tom soon spotted what was missing.
"Your silver thimble, mother, your special silver thimble!"
They searched high and low but could not find it anywhere. If you can, then you are cleverer than they.

Back they went to the police station. They found P.C. Dog up to his ears in crime.

"Four more burglaries reported!" he said glumly. "The trouble with this fellow is that he doesn't know when to stop!"

"Five," said Tilly, and told him their news. "Who else has been robbed?"

He ticked them off.

"Mr Fox, Mr and Mrs Frog, Mr Rat and Mrs Rabbit."

He wagged his head (not his tail).

"Those four were my main suspects for the Big Burglary," he said.

"I'd worked it all out. They go to town every week on the train. But now they've been robbed themselves, so they're in the clear. So WHODUNNIT?"

"Give us the list of stolen things," said Tom. "We're amazingly good spotters. We'll see if we can spot them."

So P.C. Dog gave them the list:

   Mr and Mrs Frog: One Jack-in-the-box.

   Mr Fox: One Curly Shell for Listening to the Sea.

   Mrs Rabbit: One Teapot shaped like a Cottage.

   Mr Rat: One Valuable Gold Watch on a Chain.

"What?" said Tom. "It was stolen from his pocket?"
"He kept it on the mantelpiece," said P.C. Dog. "Can't afford a clock, he says."

"Leave it to us," said Tilly. "We'll find out whodunnit."

"It's a very odd thing," said Tom. "P.C. Dog has four suspects, and those are the very people who have been burgled."
"But what if one of them *hasn't* been burgled at all?" said Tilly. "What if one of them is the real Burglar trying to put us off the scent?"
"In that case, one of those missing items was never even there in the first place," said Tom. "But which?"

That was the question.

Did Mr and Mrs Frog really have
a Jack-in-the-box?

Did Mr Fox have a Curly Shell
for Listening to the Sea?

Did Mrs Rabbit have a Teapot
shaped like a Cottage?

Did Mr Rat really have a Valuable
Gold Watch on his mantelpiece?

Tilly and Tom were stuck. They
couldn't find out.
But *you* can, can't you?
Why don't you look to see if those
things were really there?
You only have to turn the pages back.
You might find out WHODUNNIT!
If you do, keep it secret!

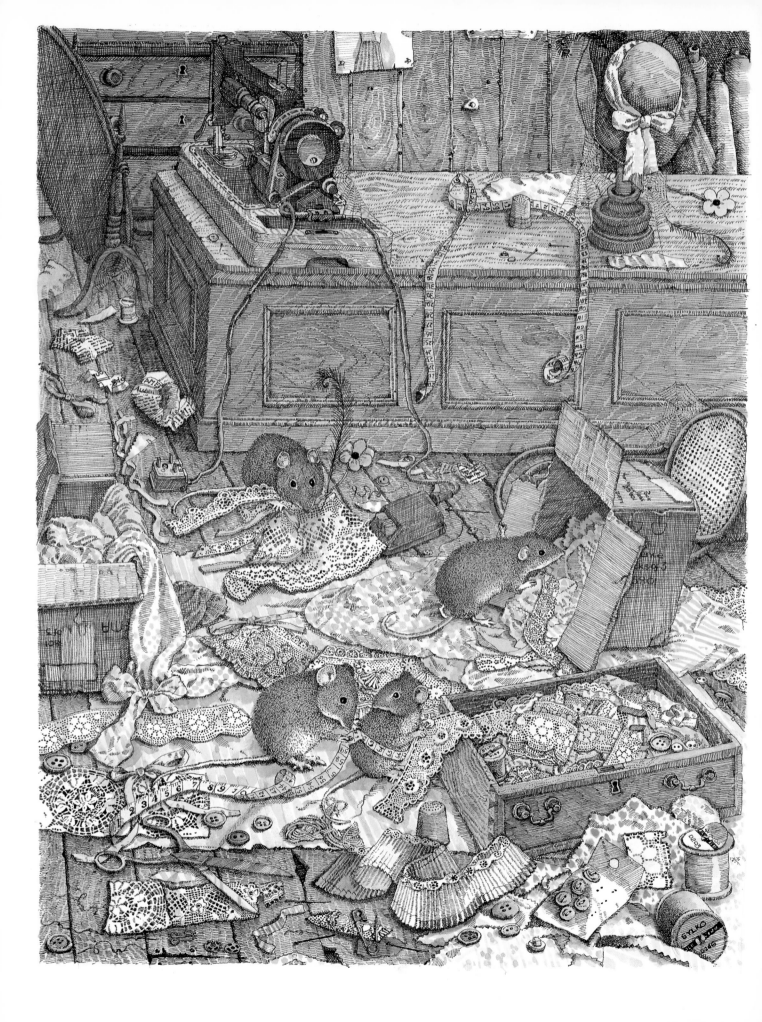

Tilly and Tom ran off home to tell the news. Their attic was littered with loops of lace. Mrs Mouse was the Village Dressmaker. She was now busy making special outfits for her own family.

Even if her special silver thimble had been stolen, everyone wanted their finery ready for the fête tomorrow.
"I'm blessed if I care whodunnit!" she cried.

The whole village was in a flummox. They were all busy getting ready for the fête, but they were all trying to guess WHODUNNIT?

The Cats were particularly nervous. Mrs Cat put all her rings and valuables into her hot water-bottle, and took it to bed with her.

"And make sure you bolt the door!" she told her husband. "Or we shall be burgled in the night!"

But one by one the lights went out in Butterly, and nobody came burgling in the deep dark night. (Unless you can spot somebody?)

Only the light in the police station burned. P.C. Dog still did not know whodunnit, so he sat up writing a notice, to make him feel better.

When day dawned he went and pinned up his notice on the Village Green.

It said:

TODAY IS A DAY
WHEN A PICKPOCKET
MIGHT PARTICULARLY
TRY TO MAKE
RICH PICKINGS
PICKING POCKETS
SO MAKE SURE *YOUR*
POCKET ISN'T PICKED.

Try saying *that* pickly –
I mean quickly!

Everyone gathered on the green to greet the Princess, and still everyone was asking the same question: WHODUNNIT?
The Burglar knows, and perhaps *you* know (but don't tell yet) and all of a sudden, Tilly and Tom know! They have spotted something!
Have you?

The Princess arrived and there was a mighty cheer. Flowers and flags flew everywhere. Tilly and Tom curtsied and bowed.
"What would you like as your reward, you amazingly clever mice?" the Princess asked.
They had been told what to say.
"Your wish shall be granted," she said. (Can you guess what the wish was?)

There was clapping and cheering.
"There is now only one question to be asked," said the Princess.
"WHODUNNIT?"

There was a little silence. The crowd held its breath.
Then,

"HEDUNNIT!"

cried Tilly and Tom together.
Everyone followed their pointing paws and saw – have you
guessed it? – Mr Rat!

He tried to bolt, but P.C. Dog was too quick for him.
"Gotcher!" he growled, and felt in his pocket for the handcuffs.
"Where…? Where…? They've *gone*!"
"HEDUNNIT!" roared the crowd.
"HEDUNNIT!"
But I expect you already knew whodunnit,
didn't you? *You* helped to solve the Big
Butterly Burglary, too. What a pity you
couldn't go to the fête!

P.S. I wonder if you guessed what the reward was? Mrs Mouse found her special silver thimble!

And is now Dressmaker by Royal Appointment!

First published 1986   Illustrations copyright © 1986 by Caroline Browne   Text copyright © 1986 by Jonathan Cape Ltd
Jonathan Cape Ltd, 32 Bedford Square, London WC1B 3EL
Printed in Great Britain by W. S. Cowell Ltd, Buttermarket, Ipswich